T0198870

GALACTIC WARRIORS
THE NEW BEGINNING

JAMES A. FLOYD

authorHOUSE®

AuthorHouse™
1663 Liberty Drive
Bloomington, IN 47403
www.authorhouse.com
Phone: 1-800-839-8640

Published by AuthorHouse 4/12/2012

ISBN: 978-1-4685-7515-6 (sc)
ISBN: 978-1-4685-7516-3 (e)

Library of Congress Control Number: 2012906196

This book is printed on acid-free paper.

1

Celebrations began to erupt throughout the Hedera Solar System as word spread of the treaty between Nebulan and Neptonia.

On Nebulan, fireworks were popping, bands were playing, and people dancing as they awaited not only the return of the Galactic Warriors but also the thousands of P.O.Ws that were being released from Neptonia. Many of whom had been captive for over five years.

On Kech, the warriors and the Neptonians were having celebrations and reunions of their own. Prince Darnell and Colonel Terry were much needed father and son time while Queen Alexandria was busy making preparations with Mariana and Regina for their wedding.

Now Captain Slaughter celebrated in a way he had been waiting forty years to do. He slipped away from the crowd and found an unused dorm room. He promptly took off his gear and helped himself to the most relaxing sleep that he's had in years. For the first time in his life, he slept with the peace of mind of knowing that he didn't have to look over his shoulder or be called to battle. For the next few hours, Slaughter would snore all of his cares away.

Captain Arnold Burns and Sergeant Major Darrell Dawson ("DD) decided to go into the streets and celebrate with the citizens of Kech. While Sergeant "Buck" Harris, always the military professional, decided to check the instruments on the shuttle and make sure everything was in working order. Many outside of the unit took him as strange, but those that knew him best would trust him with their lives. Part of his charm and personality was embedded in the fact that he was a man of few words. If he ever became talkative, that's when the warriors would look at him as strange.

Of course, as always, Corporal Akasha Jefferson was left out of the loop. With nothing to do or anyone to celebrate with, she decided to join the ladies in their wedding preparations. As soon as she walked into the room, Regina and Mariana gave her the sit down and shut up look. Akasha quickly recognized this and walked to the other side of the room and sat on the couch. She occupied herself with scientific magazines left by students from the university. She felt one day that she would measure up and be considered an equal with the rest of the group and not someone that needs a babysitter.

As everyone outside the school auditorium was celebrating, many of the elders of Kech felt that this was a day that they would never live to see; a day that saw the Neptonians and Nebulites at peace. There were large groups of people peaking through the windows of the auditorium hoping to catch a glimpse of Queen Alexandria conversing with the Regina and Mariana. The scene was almost mob like as people were pushing others out of the way in order to see this historical event. Every now and then Alexandria would go to the windows and wave at the thousands of on lookers celebrating in the streets below. In her mind, Alexandria wanted the same type of mood for her people on Neptonia. After forty years of her father's tyranny, she wanted Neptonians to be able to decide their own destiny. She was so anxious to get back to Neptonia, but at the same time wanted to continue the peace process with Nebulan and not rush anything. For Alexandria it was not only about peace, but also the healing of her family.

While looking out of the window at the celebrations, Alexandria became overwhelmed with emotions. Tears began to flow down her cheek. Noticing this, Mariana and Regina walked over to console her. She put her arm around both of them and smiled while still starring outside. Grabbing the ladies by the hands, Alexandria led them both to the center of the room.

"Akasha, sweetie, would you like to come over and join us in a word of prayer? asked Alexandria.

Immediately Akasha jumped up from the couch and grabbed Regina's hand. "Let us bow our heads." Alexandria said gently. "Father it's in the mighty name of Jesus that we come before you as boldly yet humbly as we know how. We thank you for April 15, 5012 for this is the day that will forever be known as our independence day; A day in which planets are freed and families are unified. Forgive us for the years of death and destruction caused by hate and ignorance. Fill us now with peace, love, and joy that will not only uplift your kingdom but also the entire Hedera Solar System. Finally Lord bless the unions that are about to take place. Through war we see you still bless us with love. It's in Jesus name we pray amen."

Following the prayer, they all embraced in a group hug which consisted of lots of smiles and tears.

"Your highness you got some sista in yo blood." said Akasha. I didn't know you had it like that." Regina and Mariana both turned and looked at her with their eyebrows almost raised out of their sockets. "Akasha!" But actually her words brought a smile to Alexandria's face.

"It's ok ladies. I thank God for the word that he placed in my heart and I thank him even more for allowing me to share it with you."

Alexandria put her arm around Akasha and began to change the subject. It was easy enough to recognize that she wasn't receiving much positive attention and maybe the warriors were a bit inexperienced to understand teen age psychology. But at 31 years old and a mother, Alexandria recognized what Akasha was going through.

"Ladies I want you to know that I consider it an honor and a privilege to host this intergalactic event that will forever link our worlds together." Said Alexandria.

Suddenly, without warning, a look of concern came across Mariana's face. Alexandria just reminded her of one important detail that everyone forgot in all of the excitement.

"Oh no!" Mariana yelled "What is it?" asked Alexandria. Who became even more worried as she looked at the shade of red that came across Mariana's face? "I just remembered that military marriages have to be approved by the high council and for that to happen Moses would have to part the Red Sea right in front of them." "High Council? What's the High Council? "Alexandria asked with a look of confusion. "The High Council is the military authority on Nebulan. They're made up of five highly decorated Generals and these guys literally lay down the law for the military." answered Mariana. "Oh I see." "Actually, your highness, if you can remember from your days at the academy, the law forbids marriage in the military ranks." said Regina.

Nodding in agreement, Alexandria began to pace the floor and think about the situation. Remembering the strictness of the Nebulan code, she was wondering how to address this before the council. This was a very delicate matter that had to be handled with dignity and tact.

"Well if we can survive a near Armageddon, I'm sure we can overcome the High Council." Alexandria thought to herself.

Jumping from her seat, Regina walked over towards Mariana. "Major their never going to go for our getting married. I'm sure this thought escaped the fellas also."

With these words, Mariana's face and tone became very serious. She was not about to give up on the man that she loved." Corporal how could you say that! These are the men that we love and we have to do all that we can to make this happen. "

Mariana's tone angered Regina and she quickly forgot rank and file and lashed out at Mariana. "With all due respect major! You know as well as I do that these guys are hardliners and never deviate from military regulations. I believe in fighting for my man and don't appreciate you implying otherwise. Maam!"

Mariana quickly became face to face with Regina; both starring down each other. Alexandria quickly walked between them and gave them a motherly stare which meant for them to separate. Both returned to their seats in anger.

"Ladies now is not the time to argue but to work together as a team to find a way to convince the High Council to change their minds. I believe I have an Idea on how to do this but you ladies have to get it together and follow my lead. Do you understand?" " Yes Maam." Responded Mariana and Regina; still not looking at each other or really wanting to speak.

"So what's the scoop yo highness? How we gonna get the old folks to change their minds?'" Akasha asked. In her own way was trying to lighten the mood of the conversation. "Simple, my dear Akasha." Alexandria said as she walked over towards Regina and Mariana. "I'm going to personally address the High Council on Nebulan and ask for this military article to be changed. As a matter of fact, I'm going to change this same article on Neptonia. Ladies it's not going to be easy, but you're going to have to trust me and most importantly trust God."

Alexandria sat between both of them and put her arms around their shoulders. She gave them both kisses on the forehead in order to try and restore love to the conversation. With her words and motherly tact, faith was once again restored to the spirits of Mariana and Regina. They once again could see the light at the end of the tunnel.

"Are you sure this will work?" Mariana asked. With a smile Alexandria answered. "Nothing is guaranteed in this life. But also God doesn't want us to give up on him or feel sorry for ourselves. The scripture says" With him all things are possible." It's important that you and your fiancés plead your cases before the council with determination and honor. Get the council to understand that marriage will enhance your lives and not hinder your military obligations. Understand?" Mariana and Regina both nodded in agreement. Understanding that convincing the members of the High Council to break with 150 years of tradition would be a battle in itself.

"So when are you returning to Nebulan?" asked Alexandria. "I'm not sure" said Mariana while shrugging her shoulders. "That would be up to Colonel Terry. I do know that the council is anxious for us to return and make our report." "I see. Well I have to get to a flat screen and check on things on Neptonia. But if it's all the same with you ladies, I'd like to accompany you to Nebulan and ratify our treaty in person rather than through a monitor." Smiling, Mariana walked over and sealed the deal with a hug. "Of course that's ok and I know the colonel will second that." "Great. Now if you ladies would excuse me, I have to return to my shuttle."

All eyes were on Alexandria as she gracefully left the room. Her long royal blue dress glided on the ground as she walked. The girls were secretly envious of her wardrobes and first class jewelry. They never had the opportunity to dress like ladies because of their military commitments. But just once they'd like to wear a dress with matching earrings and carry themselves like ladies and not always have to sweat like a man. Inside they were praying to get the approval of the high council. Not only for personal satisfaction, but also their future happiness was on the line.

The rest of the day passed by rather quickly and before they knew it 9p.m. had struck. The ladies were tired and rather than wait for the guys to return from partying, they decided to turn the lounge into their quarters and knock out for the evening. No more than 15 minutes after getting to sleep, the guys returned and were in rare form. Of course the ladies were awakened by their loud noises and Regina came out to investigate.

"Hey you guys are you going to wake up all of Kech? What's your problem?" said Regina. "DD" walked over to her with a big grin on his face. He always looked for a reason to raise her blood pressure and this was a great opportunity; especially in front of the other men.

"Well Corporal believe me when I tell you that there is no problem. I do believe my fellow warriors can attest to that. Aint that right fellas?" " "DD" looked over to the other men hoping to receive backup, but their instincts told them not to push Regina too far. Realizing that he was all alone, he made a slow retreat to the closet couch. Regina gave him a look of someone that was ready for action. But before she could lay into him, a transmission came over the screen.

"Someone is paging us." said Captain Barns. "On Screen" Immediately General Thomas appeared on the monitor with his normal stoic, never satisfied look on his face. "Good evening Galactic Warriors." "Good evening sir." "Where is your commanding officer?" "He's meeting with Prince Darnell sir." answered Barns. Thomas took a brief pause to evaluate the situation then continued. "I see. Well first allow me to congratulate you on bringing peace to the Hedera system. It's my understanding that you have a pretty interesting report on this matter and we are very anxious to hear it. When can we expect your return to Nebulan?"

Understanding that it was out of protocol for a person of her rank to speak out of turn, but Regina knew she had the answers that the general was looking for.

"Permission to speak sir?" said Regina. "Permission granted corporal." Regina walked over to the flat screen and began to address General Thomas. "Sir after Major Woods and I personally spoke with Queen Alexandria, we came to an agreement to conduct the treaty signing on Nebulan Tomorrow sir." "Who all were present at these negotiations?" Asked Thomas. Regina knew that the wrath of the dragon was about to come. She calmed nerves and took a deep breath before responding. "Major Woods, Myself, and Corporal Jefferson negotiated these terms sir. May I add." " No you may not add!" Thomas interrupted. "When you negotiate, you do it with your commanding officer present. And never confirm anything without him. Do I make myself clear corporal!" "Yes sir." "Captain Barns I'm trusting you to get the word to Colonel Terry and Major Woods that I want a private transmission with them within the hour." "Yes Sir" Barns responded.

With that, General Thomas cleared the transmission and left everyone alone to ponder his words. At that time "Buck" returned from making shuttle repairs and saw a look o f bewilderment on everyone's face.

"What's wrong?" "Buck" asked as he continued to scan the blank faces in the room. "Nothing is wrong sergeant" responded Barnes. "Is our shuttle ready for travel?" "Yes sir Captain. Completely ready for takeoff." The look of pride on his face when he answered let Arnold know that there was no need to complete a vehicle inspection. If there is one thing you can count on with "Buck" it was his word.

"Ok Corporal Sims go and wake up the major and Corporal Jefferson and explain to them what's going on. I'll contact the colonel. "Said Arnold "Yes sir." Regina saluted and left the room.

After giving the orders, Barns pulled his walkie from his belt. "Colonel Terry." Arnold called out. "Yes Captain." "I'm sorry to interrupt you sir but General Thomas wants a private transmission with you and the major within the hour." "Thank you captain. I shall return shortly." said Reginald. "Yes Sir. Burns out."

Everyone in the room was surprised by the attitude of the general considering they just saved thousands of lives and reunited many families with this peace treaty. For many of the warriors, their spirits were crushed and left speechless. They were left to wonder what more could they do to win the respect of the High Council.

"You know I'm not the smartest man in the world, but I don't believe the general was too happy." said "DD" "I believe you're right." said Wally sarcastically. "But seriously guys don't let this attitude diminish our historical accomplishment. We upheld the freedom of the Zartonian galaxy and more importantly the memory of our parents. This is a time of reflection and celebration.

"I agree." Reginald said as he entered the room with Prince Darnell. "What has been accomplished between Neptonia and Nebulan is nothing short of a miracle. That's something that no one can take away from us."

Mariana and Akasha entered the room sluggish from sleep. "Is everyone here?" asked Reginald as he scanned the room. Wanting everyone's attention, he moved directly to the front of the room and began to speak.

"Ladies and gentleman I want to first announce that this young man standing next to me is my son." Reginald motioned for Mariana to join them. With a big grin that overrode her sleepiness, she rose up and joined him. "This beautiful woman is my fiancé."

With these announcements, everyone applauded and whistled in celebration. This instantly changed the entire mood of the room and now everyone was ready to celebrate again. As he motioned for everyone to calm down, Reginald Continued. " First, after a very big discussion and catching up on some missed years, Prince Darnell and I have agreed to spend a great deal of time together. Also he's going to help us, with the Queen's approval of course, with military and technology trade that Nebulan and Xandar so desperately need. Also, again with the queen's approval, Prince Darnell has agreed to allow us to run training exercises on Neptonia in exchange for us helping their citizens with farming and agriculture.

Everyone was so excited about these accomplishments that they erupted in thunderous applause. This is what everyone was waiting years to hear. Everyone felt trust and ease with Reginald's words.

After once again calming everyone down, Reginald continued. " Now the young lady to my right, regardless to what the High Council says, will be my wife. I'd prefer to have the backing of the High Council, but if not, I think having my son and my wife as part of my life is not such a bad trade off."

After saying this, Reginald and Darnell joined the group in preparation for more serious discussion. Everyone was focused and ready to hear what was said. No one was thinking of anything else but the business at hand. After sitting at the table for a few moments, Reginald realized that he needed Queen Alexandria's presence for negotiations. "I tell you what everyone, the hour is late and I'm sure the queen is sleeping. Let's hammer this out the first thing in the morning before returning to Nebulan? Agreed?"

Everyone nodded in agreement and began to depart for bed. Mariana and Reginald stayed behind to prepare for their meeting with General Thomas. After giving Prince Darnell a fatherly hug, he returned to Mariana. No sooner than he sat down, General Tomas appeared on the screen.

"Good Evening Colonel Terry, Major Woods." "Good evening sir." Getting right to the point, how are negotiations with the Neptonians?" Holding back a smile from his face, Reginald responded." Sir we have a deal in principal with Prince Darnell and tomorrow we meet with Queen Alexandria to see if she agrees with the terms sir." " Well colonel why wasn't the council informed of these terms?" "Well sir we've also set up a meeting of both sides tomorrow on Nebulan in which everyone can have an input." said Reginald. "In my opinion General Thomas these terms are very attractive sir." Thomas rubbed his chin while pondering Reginald's words." It's my understanding that you were meeting with Prince Darnell while Major Woods and non commissioned officers were meeting with Queen Alexandria. Is this correct?" " Yes sir. But there is more to this situation than you know sir." "I'm sure there is Colonel Terry and before any negotiations take place tomorrow, I want that report before the High Council. Also I want to know why minor officers were involved in the negotiations with the queen of the largest empire in the Zartonian galaxy! Do you understand me Colonel Terry and Major Woods?" Thomas exclaimed.

Thomas's demeanor and voice grew angrier with each word. In his mind he believed the Neptonian Empire had taken advantage of teenaged officers and feared for the safety of Nebulan and its allies. Even in the midst of the celebrations taking place on Nebulan, Xandar, Kech, Argon, and Cortovia it seemed the greatest challenge for the Galactic Warriors would be to convince the High Council to trust their judgment.

"I want you back on Nebulan by 1300 tomorrow to meet with this council." said Thomas. "Yes sir." "Thomas Out!!"

Leaning back in the chair, Reginald and Mariana felt very disheartened. If the general treated them like this after all of their accomplishments, how could they possibly convince the High Council to allow them to marry?

With his hands clasped behind his head, Reginald took a deep breath. "Mariana." "Yes Reginald." "Something tells me we may have to put in for early retirement. I pray to the heavens above that the High Council doesn't say anything to tick off the Neptonians, because honestly, my family will always win out over career and I'm not about to lose my wife and son over their stupidity." Looking over at Reginald with sympathy, Mariana reached out and put her hand on his shoulder. "We're not going to worry but instead pray. I believe that the worse is behind us but sometimes true happiness has to be fought for. Are you ready to fight my love?" Reginald took a deep sigh and looked over at the loving eyes of his fiancé. "You know what Mariana? Yea I'm ready to fight."

2

Early the next morning as Alexandria was preparing for her meeting with the warriors, she began to get curious about her sons meeting with Reginald. The more she thought about it, the more her mother's curiosity took over. Although an important meeting was about to take place, Alexandria just had to speak to her son. She finished getting dressed and walked the hallway to his room and knocked. Looking on his monitor and seeing his mother, Darnell gathered himself to look presentable. "Come in mother." Alexandria entered the room and greeted her son with a hug and kiss on the cheek. "Have a seat." Said Darnell as he made room for her on the couch. Alexandria could see a new gleam in his eyes and renewed energy with his steps that no doubt resulted from spending time with his father.

"Thank you so much." Said Alexandria. "And how are you this fine morning?" Darnell looked over at his mother with a grin as he seated himself in front of her. "What you mean to ask is how was my meeting with father?" Darnell said with a chuckle. "Oh its father now?" said Alexandria with a look of surprise on her face. Her eyebrows rose as she moved toward the front of the chair. "Oh do tell." As Darnell was about to respond, a transmission came over the flatscreen. "Prince Darnell would you be requiring breakfast sir?" "Mother are you hungry? "Asked Darnell. "Just coffee son if it's all the same. I plan on getting full from your words this morning." " Two coffees thank you." Responded Darnell. "As you wish my prince."

Darnell jumped right back into the conversation as though there was no interruption. "Well mother we had an excellent time. I learned so much about his career, family and personality. We exchanged war stories and I learned that my grandfather was also a very distinguished war hero."

Darnell spoke with a look of pride and enthusiasm as he spoke about his father. This was something that he wanted to be able to do all of his life. His anger and desire for galactic conquest had completely subsided. His focus now was spending as much time with his father a s he could. Alexandria looked and smiled with each word from her son. This is the look that she always wanted to see on her son's face; a look of joy and happiness versus anger and frustration. Darnell was looking like a brand new man and now could finally move forward with his life.

"I can't say that I agree with your methods concerning father, but I'm so glad that you brought him into my life." Said Darnell. "Oh son I'm so sorry about that but I only did what I thought was right. I should have told you long ago." Agreed Alexandria. Darnell put his hand on her shoulder in comfort. "Mother don't worry about a thing. All is forgiven. You've been a great mother to me and great queen for Neptonia. You deserve a great amount of credit for this peace treaty. Grandfather would assume just go to his grave rather than have a peace treaty with any planet. But you mother have given Neptonia the peace that it has needed for a long time."

With that said mother and son exchanged hugs. " Son we need to be heading to the meeting room." "Yes mother I'm ready."

Captain Slaughter was waiting outside of Darnell's quarters refreshed from an entire day's rest. He felt better than he did in a long time and was ready to resume his duties. As Darnell and Alexandria exited the room, she put her arm around Slaughter. "Did you enjoy your rest Captain?" Slaughter put his head down in shame. He wasn't sure how to answer that question because it was truly new territory for him. In his mind he felt in some way that he neglected his duty as a soldier and protector of the queen.

"I apologize your highness. This...." "Not another word captain" Alexandria interrupted. "You earned and deserved that rest. Once we return to Neptonia I want you to take a weeklong vacation and any open land in my kingdom where you want to establish a household." " But my queen." Slaughter began. "No buts captain. Its queen's orders." Alexandria and Darnell gave him a slight grin for they truly appreciated Slaughters loyalty and efforts over the years.

"Thank you my queen." Slaughter said humbly. "No Captain its I that should thank you for your many years of loyal service to the Kingdom of Neptonia.

The three of them walked down the hallway towards the auditorium of the school where the meeting was to take place. Things were starting to get back to normal and students were once again shuttling back to the University and professors were settling back into work.

As Alexandria walked down the hall in her long royal blue dress and matching turquoise jewelry which consisted of earrings and rings, everyone in the hallway stopped just to get a glimpse of her. Nothing so beautiful had ever walked on Kech before and people were taking pictures and getting autographs. The women of Kech had never seen such long perfectly straight hair that went all the way down to her waist. Everyone was so impressed and surprised that the queen of the great Neptonian Empire was gracious enough to take time for the students of Kech University.

As the Neptonians were entertaining the students, the Galactic Warriors were walking toward the crowd from the opposite end of the hallway. They made their way through the crowds, shaking hands of students along the way. Once inside the auditorium, everyone took their seats at the makeshift negotiating tables.

Everyone on Kech knew the importance of this meeting and how this day would change their lives forever.

As the Neptonians made their way into the auditorium, they shook hands with the warriors and exchanged greetings.

"Let us bow our heads in prayer" said Alexandria. "Father as we come together today, bless us with wisdom, love and peace in our hearts. Let us leave here with the understanding that we are all God's children and we are to love one another. We pray for the Zartonian Galaxy and please let us not forget the lives that were lost so that this day would be possible. In Jesus Name Amen."

" Let me begin by saying that me and Major Woods had a meeting with General Thomas last night and he informed me us that we're to be back in Nebulan by 1300" said Reginald. "Ok it's now 8:30 so that gives us around 4 hours to complete these negotiations" said Prince Darnell as he looked at the time on the flatscreens. Taking out her notescreen, Alexandria gave Darnell a look of readiness. "Ok who's going to begin?" asked Alexandria. "Colonel Terry and I agreed in principal on some important issues that I'd like to present to you my queen." Alexandria nodded and Darnell proceeded.

"My queen the first area that we'll address is trade. Agriculture is an area that is lacking for the citizens of Neptonia but Nebulan has agreed to allow teams of agriculture professors from Argon to come and educate our citizens in this area in exchange for weapons technology. We would also allow military training exercises on Xandar and Neptonia."

After completing his presentation, he looked over to Alexandria for input. She completed typing her notes then looked toward Reginald.

"Well I'm in agreement that the climate on Neptonia makes farming very difficult. Our people need to be educated in this area. How would this education process take place colonel?"

Reginald pulled a chip out of his briefcase and placed it in the side of the flatscreen. Instantly images of farming villages and cities appeared on a hologram in the middle of the table. The images were very 3 dimensional and life like which completely captured the attention of everyone.

"We want to send educators from Argon here to our farming provinces to the south of Kadesh. I believe it would be important for them to physically teach Neptonians the exact principles from crop planting to maturity. Your climate is very difficult but we are confident that can make this program work.

Reginald pointed at the diagram in lecturing fashion to emphasize his point. Seeing that he had everyone's attention, he continued.

"In short we want the citizens of Neptonia to feel confident as they raise crops to feed their families. We understand for many that farming has been a way of life for generations. That's why in addition to these teachings, we would like to set up farmer markets where farmers can sell their crops for an additional profit for their families as well as for the kingdom in the form of taxes."

"So who would operate these markets?" said Alexandria as she was typing her notes. "Well your highness in the beginning we would assist the citizens with the foundation and framework of business ownership. Once they're comfortable, then they would take full responsibility for the profit margin of their business. If successful, this would create jobs as well as revenue for the province and kingdom."

Alexandria looked over at Captain Slaughter. "What do you think Captain?" He looked at her in surprise because her father never asked his opinion on anything. After overcoming the initial shock, he gathered himself then spoke. "Well my queen our people need education in many areas and I believe the colonel's proposal will give farmers a sense of pride and accomplishment." Alexandria nodded in agreement as she read her notes. "Colonel I agree with this. I believe we could all benefit from this" said Alexandria. "And what would be the format for training exercises?"

Reginald looked over at Mariana and Arnold and nodded. "I'm going to let Major Woods and Captain Barnes gives you those details."

Mariana and Arnold walked to the front of the room carrying folders and notes. "With your permission your highness, we have three phases to this plan" said Mariana. "First we are going to enlarge our military academy on Nebulan in order to accommodate cadets from Neptonia. We would like for cadets to not only experience military drills on Nebulan, but also Neptonia. This will build a sense of unity and realism for the trainees." " Who would fund this expansion Major?" asked Darnell. "Good question" responded Mariana. "We're praying that the High Council grants us the 5,000 credits needed to complete this project."

Darnell and Alexandria exchanged glances then he whispered in her ear. Alexandria nodded in agreement. "Major since this is a joint project, we feel that it's only fair that Neptonia contribute 2500 credits and any additional weaponry that you need" said Alexandria

With a look of relief, Mariana smiled then looked towards Reginald who nodded in agreement. "Thank you so much your highness. Your generosity is greatly appreciated. I'll let captain Barns give you the remainder of the plan" said Mariana.

"Thank you Major Woods" said Arnold. "Your highness we'd also like to propose joint military exercise on Cortovia and Xandar as well as Neptonia because we feel in the years to come that it will be important to have unity in our military. Honestly we don't know where the next threat may come from."

Arnold looked around the room expecting questions or comments but when none were given he continued.

"These exercises would take place twice per month at various locations." "Who would oversee these operations?" asked Darnell " It would be a joint venture commanded by non commission officers from both planets" answered Arnold. " I see" said Darnell. " In case of a threat from an outside force, how would we coordinate our response?" "Good question. Colonel Terry would you like to answer that?"

Rising from his chair, Reginald walked towards the front of the room. "Yes Arnold I would be happy to answer that. Prince Darnell keep in mind that Kech is our science and technology planet. We plan to build a state of the art radar system that coordinates Nebulan and Neptonia on one link. There will be joint patrols between Cortovia and the edges of the Hedera Solar System. We feel that this will be enough of an early warning system to confront any surprise attacks. But we need your help programming and installing this type of technology."

Alexandria glanced at Slaughter then to Darnell, pondering Reginald's words. "Of course you have the full cooperation of the empire colonel" said Alexandria.

The Negotiations continued another 2 hours until all details were discussed and agreed upon. Not a cross word was said or threats given. In spite of their youth, the Galactic Warriors stayed poised and showed a great amount of wisdom during this time. The Neptonians came away impressed and found a new respect for this young group. Their talent, discipline, and attention to detail were greatly admired by all.

"So are we done here colonel?" asked Alexandria. "It appears so your highness" Answered Reginald. "Corporal Sims and Corporal Jefferson are going to type the terms of the treaty and you can then look it over. If everything is in order, we'll sign the treaty before the High Council at 1500 hours on Nebulan." "Won't the High Council have to give final approval?" asked Darnell. "Yes they will. But we don't foresee any problems with that. We believe they trust our judgment" said Reginald.

Alexandria rose up from her chair visibly drained from the long negotiations. "Ok its settled. We will meet you in the city of Quetal at 1500 hours. When the treaty is finalized, please send it by Captain Slaughter" said Alexandria. "Yes your Highness" responded Reginald.

The Neptonians returned to their shuttle while the warriors remained in the auditorium for lunch and to finalize the treaty. It had been a long morning for everyone, but in the back of the warriors' mind was the chore of convincing the High Council of the terms; not to mention convincing them to allow marriage between officers. It was indeed a heavy weight for the warriors, but in their minds they were determined to see everything through.

As everyone finished their meals and returned to their rooms to pack, crowds began to gather in the launch bay. People wanted to get as close as possible to witness history in the making. As the warriors made their way to the shuttle, they couldn't help but to stand and admire the look on everyone's faces. Looks of joy and relief had come to the citizens of Kech. Now the Warriors and Neptonians were headed to Nebulan to make everything official.

"Well guys as nice as this is, we must get back to Nebulan with all haste" said Reginald. "But let us not forget what was accomplished here because this will be our legacy."

Reginald quickly turned towards Akasha. "Corporal Jefferson takes a copy of the treaty to Captain Slaughter for the Neptonian approval." "Yes sir" Akasha answered.

Akasha hurried over to Slaughter and presented him with the treaty. He in turn handed it over to Alexandria. The three of them looked thoroughly through the computer monitor at each detail. After a few minutes, Alexandria nodded towards Akasha, who then returned to Reginald.

"Colonel it meets with the Neptonian approval sir." "Very good Corporal Jefferson, Lets head home" said Reginald.

Having completed their tasks on Kech, everyone was so happy to finally get back to Nebulan. Not too much was said but everyone was thinking the same thing and asking the same question: Was their greatest battle ahead of them? Convincing the High Council would be no easy task.

3

"Colonel we're on our final approach to Nebulan" said "Buck" "Seeking permission to land in Quetal." "Very good Sergeant"

"Buck" made a final check on his radar system then opened up a hailing frequency to Nebulan. "This is Sergeant Harris of the Galactic Warriors seeking permission to land in Quetal, copy?"

After a few moments a voice responded. "This is Sergeant Krenshaw of Quetal Air force Base. Continue present speed and heading Sergeant Harris. Permission granted and welcome home." "Thank you sir" responded "Buck"

With that, everyone on the ship erupted in cheers and celebrations. The feeling of finally being home again and able to celebrate their accomplishments brought the warriors overwhelming joy and relief. There were hugs, handshakes, and kisses all around. Reginald held his arms up to get everyone's attention.

"Ladies and gentleman as we prepare to celebrate with our fellow Nebulites, remember this one's for our parents who made the ultimate sacrifice so that this day would be possible. Let us bow our heads and give a moment of silence in their honor."

Bowing their heads in silence, each person was alone with their own personal thoughts. As they remembered, some had tears rolling down their cheeks, while others had smiles. This is the day they waited all of their lives for; to be able to return home in peace.

"Amen" said Reginald "Oh there's going to be a party tonight!!" Wally abruptly yelled while giving out high fives. "Party at Wally's house!" screamed "DD" as he kissed Regina on the cheek. She in turn gave him a big hug and whispered in his ear. "I'm so proud of you." "Thanks Regina. That truly means a lot."

"Guys sorry to break this up but we're making our final approach and I need everyone to strap in" said "Buck"

"Shuttle Trinity you're clear for landing on Pod 24" said Sergeant Krenshaw. "Thank you Sergeant. Making our final decent to Pod 24." Answered "Buck"

As they landed, the Galactic Warriors were greeted by thousands of Nebulites that had waited all day for their arrival. There were cheers, music, dancing, and overall relief for this day. As the Warriors exited the ship, they were greeted with hugs, handshakes, and kisses. Everyone wanted the opportunity just to be in their presence or even touch their uniform. Then the crowd began to chant "Warriors!, Warriors!, Warriors!" Smiles were on the faces of the warriors as they reunited with the people they hadn't seen in years.

People didn't care about the rain nor the cold; all they cared about was their freedom.

It was a slow process for the warriors to make their way through the crowds to the High Council assembly building. After about an hour, they finally made it to the entrance were security personnel were waiting to escort them to the High Council. After taking a last look at the crowd and the thousands of banners/decorations, the warriors followed their escort into the elevator.

"What Floor?" said a computerized voice from the elevator. "Number 5" answered one of the security personnel.

The elevator quickly ascended and the doors opened to the council meeting chambers where the High Council was already assembled. The warriors entered in single file from highest to lowest rank and came to attention before the council.

"You may be seated" said General Thomas." Let it be noted that on this day April 16, 5012 that the Galactic warriors are assembled before myself, General Robert Thomas, General Jessica Jones, General Tony Lewis, General Rebecca Walters, and General Aaron Gordon."

The warrior's attention was completely fixed on the council. They truly didn't know what to expect but were prepared for anything. Their prayer was that the council approves the treaty without any delays and holdups.

"Are you in possession of the treaty Colonel Terry?" asked General Walter. "Yes Maam" responded Reginald as he reached into the briefcase and pulled out his computer pad. He approached the council and presented them with treaty, and returned to his seat.

Each council member studied the treaty with great detail. After a great deal of discussion and whispering, they addressed the warriors.

"Before voting on this treaty, there are questions that the council would like to ask" said General Thomas. "First, Colonel Terry do you feel that the Neptonians can be trusted to keep their end of the treaty?" "Yes general" said Reginald as he stood at attention. "To a man we feel the Neptonian Empire can be trusted with the terms of the treaty sir."

The council members then looked down at General Gordon and nodded. "Galactic Warriors I personally have reservations about this. In my opinion I feel we're giving them too much access to our allied planets and setting ourselves up for an easy takeover. We're being too trusting of an empire that just recently was hell bent on total annihilation."

"General Gordon I understand your concerns and reservations. But I'm completely confident that the Neptonian Empire is just as committed to peace and the security of the Hedera Solar System as we are." " What makes you so confident? "Asked Gordon. " Colonel Prince Darnell wanted to finish what King Barbas had started. He hated everything Nebulan stood for and now all of a sudden he wants to be prince charming. I'm not buying it Colonel Terry."

Mariana became infuriated at General Gordon's tone and the fact that the council didn't trust their judgment. "Permission to speak sir" said Mariana. "Permission denied Major" said Thomas quickly and in an angry tone. "We only want to hear from your commanding officer is that clear?" "Yes sir" said Mariana. "This order also goes for the rest of you as well." "Yes sir" the warriors responded.

This outburst seemed to change the mood of the meeting. Calm now turned into third degree interrogations and increased pressure from the council.

"Colonel Terry, do you understand that all negotiations are supposed to be cleared through this council?" asked General Lewis. "Yes sir I understand this but I felt compelled to proceed with the negotiations because a rapport had been established" said Reginald "A Rapport?" General Lewis asked. "Yes Sir. As the report states, Captain Slaughter contacted us initially to set up a meeting between the officers of our unit and the senior leaders of the Neptonian Empire. After much discussion, we decided to accept the officers' only meeting on Kech. Before negotiations began, there were certain facts brought out that established a friendly foundation which lead to the treaty before you today" said Reginald. "Would you care to elaborate on these facts colonel?" asked General Jones. "If it's all the same with the council, we prefer to elaborate after the treaty vote maam."

The generals conferred with each other on this unusual request. There was a thin line between disrespect and understanding. The council was determining if Reginald had crossed it.

"Colonel its agreed that we shall defer these facts until after the council vote." said General Thomas. "But keep this in mind mister these facts had better be worthy of going against military regulations for negotiations." "Yes sir" Reginald responded. "Also warriors we've decided to hold off on a vote until we meet with the Neptonians. There are some important issues here that we'd like to discuss directly with them. You're dismissed until 1500 hours at such time we'll require only senior officers at these negotiations. That is all!!" said Thomas.

The council then filed out of the room while the warriors stood at attention.

Everyone was stunned at what they just experienced. The warriors were sure these negotiations would be open and shut but now face the possibility of losing all of the ground that was gained on Kech. They also felt powerless and unappreciated for their efforts, not to mention confused.

"What just happened here?" asked Mariana. "They just cut us down to pieces. They made everything we did seem so insignificant." "I agree" said Arnold. "We bring freedom to this planet and what do we get in return? If they aren't careful they're going to put us right back where we started."

Reginald stood off to himself in deep thought. Pondering the new direction of the situation and wandering if he should contact the Neptonians so they also wouldn't be caught off guard. He didn't want anything to happen that would ruin the relationship of the two planets nor with his son. Reginald was very confused about what the next course of action would be.

"Hey baby are you ok?" asked Mariana. "Yes I'm ok. Just confused about what to do next. The council doesn't understand the true nature of the situation." "No they don't Reginald and that's why you have to explain it to them. No matter what happens I'm going to stand by your side. You know what has to be done. Just do it" said Mariana.

After giving him a hug and kiss on the cheek, Mariana addressed the others in the hopes of calming their minds.

"Is everyone ok?" asked Mariana as she looked around at everyone. "No maam we're not ok." Said "Buck". "In my opinion we were walked on today and I feel we deserved better." "I agree 100%" said Regina. "They weren't there and don't know about the camaraderie and love that was in that room on that day. They make the Neptonians out to be monsters and they're not. Maybe they were once ruthless but it was under different leadership. I don't know about anyone else but I can't sit back and watch the council destroy what we completed."

"DD" walked over and put his hand around her shoulders as she cried. Regina was angry and hurt because she felt there was no way the council would grant them permission to marry.

"What do we do?" said Wally "How do we convince the council to ratify the treaty and give permission to marry all in one day? With the way their thinking it's going to be nearly impossible."

"Ok warriors enough feeling sorry for ourselves" said Reginald as he approached the group with renewed purpose and energy. "We won the battle now it's time to win the war. Are you with me?"

Everyone came together in a huddle with all eyes on Reginald. "Watcha got in mind?" asked Akasha "Glad you asked" said Reginald. "Listen it's important that we get in contact with Alexandria before they arrive so we can join forces against the council. " " What do you mean?" asked "Buck" " I mean we need to get Alexandria to explain to the council why the treaty is important and also at the same time get the respect that we deserve" said Reginald. "So what's the plan?" asked "DD" "The plan is this; we meet over at the conference room at the academy and get in contact the Neptonians. And tell them exactly what happened. Then we take the biggest gamble of our lives and let them do all of the talking" said Reginald.

After their meeting, they quickly filed out of the room and made their way to the shuttle bay. After boarding, they quickly sped off towards the academy. It was imperative that they make contact with Alexandria immediately. The warriors made haste in getting the flatscreen set up for transmission.

"Sergeant Krenshaw set up a transmission to the Neptonians asap" said Reginald. "Yes sir colonel"

In a matter of minutes, Captain Slaughter appeared on the screen.

"Greetings Galactic Warriors; how may I be of service to you?" "It's important that we speak with Queen Alexandria prior to your arrival. It's truly an urgent matter that we have to discuss" said Reginald "Stand by. I will notify the queen at once" said Slaughter.

Once Alexandria arrived, Reginald explained the complete situation to her. He told her that the High Council reaction was completely different than expected and that the judgment of the Galactic Warriors was being called into question.

They didn't want to lose the trust and respect of the Neptonians.

After listening to the Galactic Warriors, Alexandria took a moment to ponder the situation. She understood that the situation must be handled with extreme delicacy and tact because there was a great deal of anger coming from all sides. Somehow this must be diffused.

"Ok Galactic Warriors I have an idea but no time to explain" said Alexandria. "You'll just have to trust me and follow my lead during negotiations. For those that aren't allowed to present, wait outside the door for my signal." " Yes maam" The Warriors answered.

After signing off, everyone returned to the shuttle. It was less than an hour before the meeting was to begin, so the warriors set a course to return to the High Council Quarters. Once they arrived they immediately made their way to the meeting area. The crowds outside were still heavy due to the anticipated arrival of the Neptonians. No one could rest easy until the treaty was signed and ratified by both sides. Everyone had a nervous excitement. People were happy yet reserved until the entire process was completed.

Regardless of the cold and rain, people stood their ground and waited. They understood that this wait not only meant peace, but also jobs and other opportunities for the citizens of Nebulan. Cleanups had to be done and repairs had to be made on Nebulan as well as Xandar, Argon, and Cortovia. To restore the planet's beauty, luster, and pride will take a great deal of time; probably years but everyone was anxious to get started.

It was now 14:45 and the High Council had begun to file into the chambers. At that same moment, an announcement was being made in the building." Attention! This is Sergeant Krenshaw and I'm proud to announce the arrival of the Neptonians on Pod 22. Thank You!"

With that announcement, the High Council took their seats and began to get their notepads in order. They had changed into their military best in preparation for this very important meeting. In a surprise move, the High Council also invited the Governors of the allied planets; a move that completely surprised the warriors. As the governors took their places, General Thomas addressed the warriors.

"As we prepare to greet our visitors from Neptonia, I want to remind you that this meeting is for commissioned officers only. Any non-commissioned officers may leave at this time."

Regina, "Buck", "DD", and Akasha all filed out of the room and waited in the lobby. As they took their seats, they saw the Neptonians enter the chamber with a large military escort. Queen Alexandria looked over in their direction and winked; as if to remind them of her words. The Neptonians were escorted to the front of the chambers and seated directly in front of the High Council. Each member walked over and exchanged greeting with the Neptonians. Afterward, the Governors exchanged their pleasantries as well. Finally the Galactic Warriors exchanged handshakes, and then it was down to business.

Alexandria rose to address the assembly.

"With the permission of the High Council, I'd like for us all to bow our heads in a word of prayer." "Yes your highness I believe that would be in order" Said Thomas.

Everyone stood and bowed their heads as Alexandria was preparing to speak.

"Most gracious heavenly father, here we are standing before you asking for wisdom, patience, and love as we prepare to unify our galaxy. We ask that your spirit guide our hearts and our words during these negotiations. Forgive our sins and bless our families. In Christ Jesus name we pray. Amen."

"First before we begin, allow me to introduce the Governors of our allied planets. From Cortovia Governor Bach Simmons, From Argon Governor Michael Kon, From Xandar Governor Adam Schilly, From Kech High

Akeem and from Nebulan William Lenny. We've invited our Governors here because we feel that their input here will be very valuable to these proceedings. Also it's important that no one is left in the dark" Said Thomas. "Also your Highness, allow me to introduce our Military High Council. Beginning to my left is General Jessica Jones, General Tony Lewis; to my right is General Rebecca Walters and General Adam Gordon. Of course you remember our Galactic Warriors."

After the introductions were made, Alexandria was given the opportunity to address the assembly first. Her beauty, along with her elegant queen attire, more than caught the attention of the assembly. Her graceful walk and waist length hair added charm and grace to her words.

"Members of the High Council, Governors, and Galactic Warriors; I'm Queen Alexandria and this is my son Prince Darnell, along With Captain Slaughter our military commander. We come before you to first offer our apologies for the ten years of bloodshed endured on both sides. My father created many enemies and separated many families. I want each person here to understand that although I loved my father, our ruling styles are completely opposite. I have a goal of peace and reconciliation for the Neptonian Empire. I want to leave a kingdom of honor and respect for my son so that he can continue on in this new legacy. We want this to be a whole galaxy again where we help and defend each other. I pray that each person here understands the importance of this day and puts politics behind them; thank you General for the opportunity to speak. "

Alexandria returned to her seat as everyone soaked in what she said.

"Let us begin shall we?" said Thomas.

Immediately Alexandria stood up and interrupted General Thomas.

" Before we get started General, I'd like to say that when we were in negotiations, we met with the entire officer core of Galactic Warriors and would respectfully ask that all be present for this meeting" said Alexandria.

The council immediately conferred with each other. After brief deliberations, Thomas addressed the questions.

"It's highly irregular for non-commissioned officers to attend these proceedings. But since they did begin the negotiation process, it's only fair that they see it through."

Thomas motioned to one of the security personnel to bring them in. As they entered, they joined the other warriors at their table. The y remembered Alexandria's words about following her lead and seemed that her planned was on the verge of beginning.

"The first order of business is that of damages incurred on Nebulan and its allied planets" said Thomas. "It's going to take thousands of credits to repair infrastructure that we just don't have. We feel that the empire has to bare some burden during this rebuilding process."

Everyone nervously awaited the response of the Neptonians. Especially the warriors because they realized that this was not a part of their previous deal and the High Council was going to press hard for reparations No one knew what Alexandria's plan was or what to expect as she prepared to address the assembly. One thing was for sure was that the warriors were hanging on her every word.

Alexandria rose from her seat and began to elegantly walk before the audience. She smiled as she prepared to address the assembly.

"High Council and distinguished allied Governors, I'm not going to bore you with any long drawn out speeches or answers. I simply want to do something that's going to make these proceedings easier for everyone. Now we can sit here all say and debate every point of this treaty, but in the end I don't think anything can be gained by this .I'm willing to concede financial reparations to each of the allied planets for post war rebuilding. We were the aggressors and are prepared to work with each planet's rebuilding plan. In addition to the agreed upon terms, we will distribute 50,000 credits to each planet and any manpower that you need. All we ask is one thing in return." "What is that your highness?" asked Thomas.

Alexandria turned towards the Galactic Warriors and smiled.

"The Neptonians and the Galactic Warriors have learned so much about each other. We are linked in a very unique way. But before I make my

request, there is something that everyone in this room needs to know.
"

Alexandria turned and walked slowly towards the warriors. Looking directly at Reginald, she motioned for him to come forward.

"When I was 13 years of age, my mother enrolled me in Nebulan's Military Academy. It was during this time that I first befriended and began a romantic relationship with Colonel Terry. One year later we conceived a child together and I was forced to return to Neptonia. Colonel Terry never knew that reason for my sudden departure nor that I had a son. Due to his career and the strictness of the military code of Nebulan, I felt it best that he never know.

At this point, the council was very puzzled and wanted to know what this had to do with the proceedings.

"Who and where is this son your highness?" asked General Jones. "I'm glad that you asked that question maam" responded Alexandria who immediately turned to Prince Darnell. "My son, would you please join us before the assembly? "

Darnell walked over and stood at his father's side.

"Ladies and gentleman here is the son that I speak of as he stands next to his father. "

At once everyone's eyes were raised and some even stood to their feet, because no one could believe that the ruthless Prince Darnell is the son of Colonel Reginald Terry. The entire room was in shock. The only ones that were calm in their seats were the warriors. Everyone else was in an uproar.

"Order! Order!" yelled General Thomas. " Everyone return to your seats."

After calm had been restored, the council immediately returned their attention back to Alexandria.

"With all due respect your highness, this is completely out of order and irrelevant" Said Thomas. "You couldn't be more wrong General" countered

Alexandria. "Nebulan, Neptonia, and the entire Hedera solar system are linked by blood; blood that has been shed and blood that now lives. Our planets are now a family and nothing can change that General."

Alexandria's voice trembled with every word as her resolve had now turned into anger. With her it was not about a treaty but about the well being of her family and kingdom. She was willing to compromise whatever it took on behalf of the warriors and her son.

"Governors and High Council as I said before the Neptonian Empire would gladly finance and provide manpower for the repair of all planets. All we ask is that you keep the treaty intact and allow for one important event to take place." " What is that your highness?" asked Thomas.

Alexandria turned towards the warriors and smiled. This is the event that everyone had been waiting for. The warriors were on edge and nervous as Alexandria walked towards them.

"Major Woods, Sergeant Major Dawson, and Corporal Sims would you please join me?" asked Alexandria.

The three walked nervously towards the front of the chambers and stood next to Reginald. Inside they knew that this would change their lives one way or another. All they could do is hold their breath and pray.

"High Council we ask that you allow these two couples to marry in exchange for the aforementioned reparations" said Alexandria.

Again everyone became unglued and shocked at the request. This was clearly against Nebulan Military Regulations.

"Completely out of the question your highness" said Thomas. "These officers understand that this is completely against military regulations and not up for debate. " "General Thomas these young men and women risked their lives for Nebulan and have lost so much because of our stupidity. Can't you reward them in some sort of way?" Said Alexandria who clearly now had lost her queen-like poise and patience.

"It's their jobs to risk life and limbs for the planet and its freedoms" said General Gordon. "We are not changing regulations for anything or anybody." "Permission to speak sir" said Reginald. "Permission granted" said Thomas. "With all due respect sir, If it's because of military regulations that I can't marry the woman that I love, then I'd like to resign my commission effectively immediately. I believe that my obligation to my future wife and son are more important than a career." " Colonel are you sure that you know what you're doing? You would give up a bright and highly decorated career for marriage?" asked Thomas.

Reginald looked over at his son and over at Mariana, who had a very shocked look on her face.

"Yes sir" Reginald responded. "As I look at my fiancé and my son, I can see all of the decorations that a man needs sir." "Sergeant Major Dawson. Do you also feel the same way?" asked Thomas.

"DD" also took a long look at Regina and stepped forward. "Yes sir I feel the exact same way."

Thomas leaned back in his chair and starred at the four of them. He had a great look of disappointment on his face but knew he had to enforce military regulations. As he was about to speak, Governor Lenny interrupted.

"Wait General. I want to say that losing this men and women would be a great disservice to the military. I for one believe that in the interest of peace, galactic unity, and love that these couples should not only be allowed to wed, but the Galactic Warriors deserve accommodations for bravery above and beyond the call of duty. " "I agree" said Governor Simmons of Cortovia. " Thousands of lives have been spared because of the courage of this young group and they should be rewarded."

One by one each governor agreed that the two couples should marry and not be dishonorably discharged from the military.

Seeing that the warriors had the backing of all the delegates, the High Council's minds were changed. Each member of the council looked at the 4 and had mixed feelings about changing a 150 year old tradition.

"Warriors I'm not sure if what I'm about to do is right or not, but for the sake of peace and unity in the Hedera Solar System, the council agrees to allow theses marriages to take place. But you must understand that your responsibilities to your job and missions can never be neglected and focus must be maintained at all times. Are we clear on this?" asked Thomas. "Yes sir!" they answered. "On the other hand as I see what has unfolded before us, I have to say that there is healing needed by all parties involved. So it's the decision of this council to accept this treaty between Nebulan and the Neptonian Empire; officially ending the Galactic war."

After speaking, the members of the High Council walked to the center of the room and sat at the table along with the Neptonians. They formally signed the treaty and thus ended the 10 years of hatred and bloodshed among these two worlds.

Outside, crowds cheered and celebrated as they watched these events unfold on the jumbotron monitor. There were hugs, smiles and tears being spread throughout the entire city of Quetal. Everyone could now focus on rebuilding lives and planets throughout the solar system.

After everything was signed, Mariana and Regina couldn't resist giving Alexandria hugs. They were so chocked up that all the three could do was cry and hold each other. Even the governors could not believe that the Queen of the Neptonian Empire was actually giving hugs to Nebulites. It was something that they would never had imagined seeing in their lifetime.

"Thank you so much your highness" said Regina. "How could we ever repay your kindness?" "Don't thank me. Thank God for allowing this union to take place. But you can do one thing for me" Said Alexandria. "What's that? "asked Mariana. "Prepare yourselves for a great wedding feast on Neptonia" said Alexandria. "Really!" said Regina with great surprise and excitement. "On Neptonia?" "Yes sweetheart. On Neptonia" responded Alexandria. "When?" asked Mariana. "Ask General Thomas how soon he will allow you to leave for your wedding" Said Alexandria.

The four of them walked over to General Thomas, who was making small talk with the Governors.

"General may we have a word please?" asked Reginald. "Yes you may. What may I do for you colonel?" "Sir we were wondering how soon we would be allowed to leave for our wedding. Queen Alexandria has allowed us the opportunity to be married on Neptonia" said Reginald.

Thomas looked at them very intently and wanted to ask them to have their wedding on Nebulan, but he relented.

"Colonel you have my permission to leave immediately. As of now the Galactic Warriors are on two weeks leave with the understanding that upon you're instantly report to me in order to execute our plan to restore our planet. Understood?" " Yes sir" "Congratulations" said Thomas as he shook Reginald's hand.

With the news, relief came over the warriors. They felt as if a heavy burden had been lifted and 2 wars had been won. Although the hardest days were ahead of them with the many months of rebuilding and restoration, they knew that together they could overcome anything.

There were celebrations inside and outside of the building. As news spread of the official treaty signing, more and more people crowded the High Council command center in hopes of getting a glimpse of everyone involved.

History was being made, lessons learned and walls shattered. But the main thing for the Hedera Solar System was that the legacy of bloodshed is finally behind them.

4

The meetings were ending and the festivities were only beginning for Nebulan. There were countless parties, parades, and other gatherings to commemorate this great day. The Galactic Warriors spent days taking pictures, signing autographs, and attending celebrations. People from the allied planets also came to get a close glimpse of the young men and women that was responsible for restoring peace to the solar system.

The warriors were really soaking in all of the attention. They were overwhelmed with gifts and well wishes that left them speechless and tired at the end of the day.

Following the treaty negotiations, the warriors informed Alexandria that they needed a week to celebrate and get their personal affairs in order before the wedding took place. It had been quite some time since they had seen their homes and there was much to cleanup in the neighborhood. Also repairs had to made to many of the flatscreens and transmission equipment that was damaged during the war.

War had truly matured the warriors and home just didn't look the same.

The warriors worked around the clock in shifts bouncing from public appearances to home repair. It was a painstaking schedule and workload but unity and camaraderie developed and bonds were established.

The future for Nebulan and its allies were looking brighter each day.

Mariana and Regina worked diligently to prepare their homes for married life. Each day brought a new level of excitement for them as they decorated their homes with military precision and didn't leave anything to chance. It was so important that they prove equal balance between wife and career. They knew that the microscope would be on them and that they could leave no stone unturned since the high Council went against regulations to allow this to happen. Not to mention many stuck their necks out on their behalf.

It was on going to be a real maturing process for the 20 year old females. They weren't able to learn a lot from their parents about womanhood and marriage, but their military training taught to not to accept or make excuses. So they did the best they could and put the rest in God's hands.

They cleaned their modest two bedroom cottages from top to bottom. They added pictures, decorative awards, and other pleasantries that made their house into a home; working with a sense of pride that they haven't had before. Not to mention finally being able to work in sweats and t-shirts versus military fatigues was an added bonus.

It was a great time for the warriors; finally peace, rest, and relaxation.

"Buck", who was by nature a loner, lived outside of Quetal in a homemade log cabin. His personality and work ethic were strictly military. Never one for making excuses or small talk, he used his leave time to repair his home and replant his fields.

Everyone understood that "Buck" was very different but very dependable. He was more of a leader by example than vocal. He could be counted on to take up a great deal of slack when others fell behind. Like Slaughter, "Buck" was completely sold out on making the military his career.

Wally, "DD", Arnold, and Reginald all decided to go into the city for lunch and discuss the wedding. They chose an old fashioned " Burger Joint" where they could finally get their teeth into some burgers and fries. After living on military meals and rations for months, they could now eat their choice of anything. They sat in a booth near a window where they could watch the shuttles and aircraft flying overhead. Watching the citizens of Quetal return to their normal routines of work and school brought a sense of pride to the guys. This is something they hadn't seen in many years and now they have the opportunity to sit back and enjoy the fruits of their labor.

Everyone in the restaurant waved and saluted them. Everywhere they went, the Galactic Warriors were treated like intergalactic heroes. The sky was the limit and they wanted to enjoy every minute of it.

"May I take your order gentleman?" said the waitress. "Yes maam

You may" said Wally. "We want 3 Nebulan burgers, 3 large fries, and 3 Virgin Toties because we're celebrating!" "What's the occasion?" Asked the waitress as she typed in their orders. "These two men here are getting married next week and I want you to put the bill on me" said Wally. "Well congratulations! You men just get yourself comfortable because I'm going to take good care of you"

The waitress then ran off with great excitement after realizing that she was waiting on celebrities.

The men resumed their comfortable positions and began some manly chit-chat. They were finally able to relax and talk as men instead of officers.

"Guys can you believe that of all people it was the Neptonians that changed the minds of the High Council?" said Arnold. "Yea tell me about it. We begged and cried but all we received were headaches and rejections. But Alexandria makes a few sexy steps in a sexy dress and everybody changes their minds." Said " DD"

Everyone erupted in laughter because the more they thought about it, the more believable it became.

"Ok guys here are your Virgin Toties and your food will be right out" said the waitress. "Anything else that I can get you during your wait?" "No maam this is plenty" answered Wally. "Guys I want to propose a toast to Reginald and "DD". I wish you many years of happiness and may your love grow each and every day." " Here! Here!" said Reginald as everyone took sips from their glasses. "You guys nervous?" asked Arnold. "Not sure about the Colonel but I have to say I am" answered "DD" "I'm 20 years old I've never learned the true duties of a husband or what it takes to be a father. My father died when I was 11 and I've been learning by trial and error every since. Of course my mother did the best that she could, but it takes a man to make a man and many of life lessons I missed out on." " Well let me tell you something "DD". As long as you love that woman and do right by her, I promise God will bless you with all the wisdom that you need" said Reginald. "Yea I'm a little nervous, but considering everything that we've been through I think that it's safe to say we can overcome anything" "I agree "said Wally as he raised his glass. " To overcoming"

The men sat, ate and drank for hours. There was plenty of laughter and cheer during their celebration. It was a true boy to men moment and everyone could see the happiness and relief in these men's faces. There was an unbreakable bond being formed; one that would last a lifetime.

"Ya'll won't some help?" said Akasha as she entered the front door of Regina's house.

Regina and Mariana had been helping each other decorate and clean all week. Finally they were putting the finishing touches on their new homes. They listened to classic love music while they worked which kept them focused on what was ahead of them.

"Of course you came when we're almost done" said Regina. "Yea the only thing left for you to do is watch" said Mariana. "I guess you can help me prepare dinner. "I guess" responded Akasha; who shrugged her shoulders at the suggestion." What we eatin?"

Mariana walked towards the kitchen and studied the computer menu.

" I don't know. What are you in the mood for Regina?" " Honestly I'm in the mood for anything that doesn't walk or talk. In other words it doesn't matter. Just surprise me" said Regina, who had stretched out on her couch.

Mariana studied the list up and down then came to a decision.

"Computer. Dinner of baked chicken, mashed potatoes, and dinner rolls." " Preparation time 5 minutes" responded the computer. "Akasha can you please put in a program for chocolate cake?" asked Mariana. "Sure thing my 26th century Martha Stewart" replied Akasha.

Mariana gave Akasha a sarcastic look then rolled her eyes. Akasha, who truly was not shy, returned the favor.

Mariana returned to Regina's company before any trouble started. Both slumped back on the couch and relaxed their cares away as they watched a movie on their flatscreen.

"Well it's all over now but the walk down the aisle" said Regina. "We've done all we can do to our houses, now we have to work on us." "Well Alexandria said she would handle everything from wardrobe to makeup. The only thing that we have to do is prepare for the honeymoon" said Mariana. "Oh yes Mariana" Said Regina as she fell further back into her imagination. "I can't believe a whole week on beautiful Argon. Fun in the sun girlfriend!" " Yes Gina I can't wait. The guys already reserved the space needles overlooking the ocean and beach. So romantic" said Mariana who was starring into the ceiling envisioning the location.

"Sounds kinda dull to me" said Akasha. "The only person that needs sun is Mariana. Regina is already charcoal"

Mariana and Regina looked at each other shaking their hands. They understood who they were dealing with and just let her comments pass.

"You'll understand when you're older sista girl. Right now you're only 15" said Regina. "You're going to live with me and DD and we're depending on you to take care of the place while we're gone. Can you handle that?" "Yes I can handle that Mrs. Thang. Just leave me enough credits and food programs to get me through the week" said Akasha sarcastically. "If you need help with anything, Arnold and Wally are right down the street. Speaking of which, let me hit the Walkie and see if our men have made it home" said Regina.

Regina reached onto the table and grabbed her warlike.

"Hey "DD" where are you sweetie?"

After a brief pause he responded.

"Believe it or not we're just leaving the restaurant. What are you doing?" "You guys were at the Restaurant 4 hours? My goodness! You know that we can't get fat and lazy in these 2 weeks" chuckled Regina. "I know Gina baby but we did more laughing and talking than eating. But we're headed back home now to finish packing. How was your afternoon?" " Well we put the finishing touches on our new home and did some packing as well." Hope you guys like what you see but of course not until after the honeymoon" said Regina. "Yea Yea! Pasado de moda as the 20th century Spaniards used to say" said "DD"

"That's right. I'm old fashioned and 20th century to the heart" said Regina while laughing. "Well hey you guys be safe and we'll see you in a couple of days." "Ok. Tell Mariana that Reginald will warlike her from the shuttle in a few minutes" said "DD" "Ok. Gina out"

After the conversation, the ladies reclined back and resettled into their movie.

"Dinner is prepared" said a computer voice from the kitchen.

They went in and began to set the table for dinner. They were really more tired than hungry, but knew they had to eat something. But of course Akasha could be counted on for unwanted conversation. She always would speak when others really wanted silence or to be left alone with their thoughts.

"Ya'll bet not come back with no babies. I ain't no nanny" said Akasha.

Mariana and Regina were both too tired to acknowledge her comment. They just glanced at her and continued eating. But in the back of their minds they knew that she was going to be a handful because Akasha had so much maturing ahead of her. All Regina and Mariana wanted to do was eat and sleep.

"Well I can take a hint" said Akasha. "I'm going to my room and watch a movie. " Good. Jam your door from the inside" said Regina.

"Anyway!" responded Akasha as she made her way down the hall.

It was a welcomed relief that she left the room because Regina and

Mariana wanted to enjoy peace and quiet as well as talk about life after the wedding. They were very excited but cautious in their thinking. Years of war and witnessing death and destruction truly robbed them of their childhood innocence. The simple pleasures of games and school were exchanged for military and war. Growing up for the warriors had to be fast because loosing focus was the difference between life and death.

But what war could never be destroyed was love. The love that these men and women have for each other survived many things that people didn't. Love kept them focused and ironically love brought peace to the Zartonian Galaxy. This was a great time for reflection of their young lives. The torch had been passed to them and they took pride in how they carried it. The road had not been easy for the warriors but the experiences that they shared would give them wisdom for the rest of their lives.

On Neptonia, Queen Alexandria was working to restore trust and unity in her kingdom. She and her top advisor were meeting with rebel leaders, governors and mayors in Neptonia's capital city of Kadesh. This was an important time in the history of the Neptonian Empire. Never before had political meeting or other gatherings taken place in the royal palace. It was truly a new day for the citizens of Neptonia. Everyone in Kadesh was excited that the day they had prayed years for had finally come. The rule of tyranny had come to an end and freedom was upon them. Some even noticed that for once the sun was shining a little brighter and food tasted a little better.

Crowds were allowed to gather in the streets for festivities and other celebrations. No one could remember when there was more joy and happiness in the Neptonian Empire.

In the palace, Queen Alexandria, along with the entire rebel leaders and dignitaries were hammering out terms of a peace agreement. Because of the importance of the meeting, Alexandria spared no expense in making sure that all of her guests received the best in food, accommodations, and assigned personal servants. No stone was left unturned or request unheeded as the Empire practiced a new open door policy between the palace and the leaders of Neptonia.

It was the first time for many to even be inside of the royal palace. Everyone was so surprised to be received with open arms. And to view all of the vast decorations that were laid out in their honor. Servants, food, and music were all a part of the welcoming. Even the once hot headed Prince Darnell gave guided tours to the surprise of many.

Many changes had taken place during the week. It was the beginning of a reunification within the empire. Although great steps were beginning to be taken, everyone knew that there was still a long road ahead. There were a great number of obstacles to be removed and trust was still a major issue. Yet it was Alexandria's goal to make Neptonia into a democracy that would be an example to the Hedera Solar System.

As all 50 delegates came to their sets around the meeting tables, Alexandria made her entrance surprisingly dressed in royal blue military fatigues. Her choice of clothing caught everyone by surprise; including the usually no nonsense Captain Slaughter, who had to do a double take before being seated.

But her wardrobe was clearly sending the message that although she was queen, the needs of the empire were more important. Also absent was her normal array of jewelry and makeup but ever present was the waist length black hair and inviting blue eyes; not to mention the attention getting 5'10 stature. She was dressed for battle and this immediately received the respect of everyone in the room.

"I want to begin by saying welcome to each and every one of you. I consider it a true God-given honor and privilege to be in the presence of the men and women that will help restore unity and democracy to the Neptonian Empire. It's important that we come to the understanding that the needs of the citizens come before any personal agendas. It's important to also note that a queen is only as strong as her loyal subjects. It's best that any of you that don't feel that you can show loyalty to me or the empire, resign your positions now. Why? You may ask? Because like my father, I will deal with disloyalty very harshly. Do we understand each other?" asked Alexandria. "Yes your highness" everyone answered. "Great! Before we begin lets bow our head in a moment of prayer" said Alexandria.

"Most gracious heavenly father, we simply pray for wisdom and unity as we attempt to restore this kingdom for your people. Forgive our sins and fill our hearts with love. In Jesus name, amen"

"Ok Prince Darnell would you begin please?" "Yes my queen' answered Darnell. " First I'd like to address the leaders of the rebellion Captain Clark and Captain Jessup."

Darnell took a deep breath then continued.

"Men, regrettably battles have been fought and lives lost on both sides. But now we're asking that we go forward together and not as separate entities. As you know the treaty calls for the Nebulites to establish a military base here on Neptonia. Would you be willing to work with the Nebulites during training exercises and also train under Captain Slaughter on a full time basis?" " My prince, we have no problem working with the Nebulites on behalf of the empire" said Captain Clark. "All we ask is that our input be respected on military matters" "So noted" said Darnell. "You and Captain Slaughter will oversee military operations with the understanding that Slaughter has the final decision." "Agreed" said Captain Jessup. "Very good. It's important to understand that we not only need to work with each other but also the entire Hedera Solar System. Also our governors and mayors need to teach our citizens how to be independent in order to jumpstart our lagging economy" said Darnell.

Darnell took a drink of water and gathered himself; then continued.

"Believe me I understand that after years of living in tyranny, our people will show a great deal of mistrust, confusion, and in some cases aggression. But we must be patient and understanding because none of these changes will come overnight. It's going to take months if not years of hard work, training, dedication, and most importantly prayer in order to change the image of the Neptonian Empire and win the trust of our people. With the help of the agricultural and scientific experts from Kech and Xandar, our citizens will learn how to be self sufficient and open their own businesses. This will not only boost our economy but the overall moral of our people.

As Darnell continued to speak and educate the political leaders of

Neptonia, Alexandria couldn't help but be moved at the complete change in attitude and demeanor of her son. Gone was the quick temper and kill first mentality. Also gone was his beard and shoulder length hair. Now he carried himself with a clean shaven face and short wavy hair that made him look more like a prince than the blood thirsty man that he once was. This change was noticed by everyone in the kingdom. People didn't understand what brought about this change but it was a completely welcomed sight.

As Alexandria looked on, she noticed that she couldn't keep herself from smiling and showing pride in the man that he was becoming. It was truly hard for her to keep a professional etiquette but somehow she maintained composure.

"I know my kingdom and my son are going to be alright now." Alexandria thought to herself. She looked around and saw that everyone was focused and impressed with the plans that Darnell wa laying out.

"So are we in agreement as to the direction of the New Neptonian Empire?" asked Darnell as his eyes scanned around the room.

Everyone was in unanimous agreement with what was laid out before them. Not out of fear or any type of scare tactic, but from their freewill. Change and democracy had finally come to Neptonia.

"Before we adjourn, I want to say that it's my duty, my honor, and my privilege to announce that this Saturday my father will be getting married right here at the royal palace at 2pm" said Darnell

With that announcement, shock and amazement immediately hit the room because news had not yet spread about Darnell's reunion with his father. Darnell could see the amazed look in everyone's eyes and quickly realized that no one was aware of what happened on Kech.

"Well ladies and gentleman, in the coming weeks there will be further explanations concerning this situation. But for now just know that me and my mother would consider it a great honor for you to attend this once in a lifetime event." Darnell's face lit up and his stature more firm with the words of this announcement. Alexandria walked up and put her hand on his shoulder.

"Yes my friends we would consider it an honor if you all sit with us in the royal section of the church"

The meeting concluded with Darnell receiving many handshakes and well wishes. After everyone dispersed from the room, Alexandria, Darnell and Slaughter were left alone to soak in the atmosphere of what just happened.

Leaning back in her chair, and feet propped back on the table, Alexandria was as relaxed as she'd ever been. She looked up at the ceiling and began to lose herself in all of the paintings of past kings and queens of Neptonia. This brought up thoughts of her parents and wishing they could witness this day.

"Guys I wish my parents were alive to see the new empire. What do you think they would say" asked Alexandria. " I'm sure grandmother would be proud of you but grandfather wouldn't have any part of it" responded Darnell. "I wish grandfather would have changed his thinking before he died, but I guess it wasn't mean to be."

"How about you dear Slaughter; what are your thoughts?" asked Alexandria.

Of course loyalty and his duty first mentality made him reluctant to answer such a question. Slaughter served under King Barabas for 40 years. Although he personally didn't agree with the King's mindset, disobeying orders was not an option. Neither was speaking against the king.

"My queen this is a new day for Neptonia and I'm very honored to have lived to see this moment. But my queen I'm just a hired hand that served your father the best that I could and I pray for the strength to give you and the prince the same loyalty" said Slaughter.

Alexandria and Darnell looked at each other and began to chuckle because they knew that this was going to be the best answer that Slaughter was going to give.

"Mother I must go and contact father before bed." Will you be ok?" asked Darnell. "Yes my son. I will be fine" answered Alexandria.

After giving Alexandria a hug and a kiss, Darnell hurried to his chambers to make his transmission.

"Did you see that Captain? Now that was a true Prince that just walked out of here" Said Alexandria proudly. "Yes my queen. The prince has truly come a long way in a short amount of time. A great soldier and now a great man" complemented Slaughter. "Indeed. So dear friend have you completed your new home?" asked Alexandria.

"Yes my queen. I want to truly thank you for your generosity. The land that you've given me perfectly suits my needs" said Slaughter. "Well dear friend you deserve that and much more. You've given the empire victories, service, and most importantly loyalty. Anything you need just say the word" said Alexandria.

Slaughter walked over to Alexandria and knelt to one knee.

"It's my honor to serve you and our kingdom my queen."

Alexandria smiled as she reached down and put her hand on his shoulder.

"Rise dear friend. The hour is late. Go home and take your rest for tomorrow is a day of preparation for Regina and Mariana. There will be a great deal of work for us to do." said Alexandria

After Slaughter left, Alexandria returned to her chambers. She noticed that her hand maiden had placed new satin sheets on her bed along with sleeping attire. After changing, she called in hand maidens to style her hair for the next day's events. As Alexandria was getting her hair brushed, she couldn't help but wonder when her big day would come when one day she would bring a king to Neptonia. But Alexandria was in no hurry. In her mind the needs of her kingdom came before the matters of the heart. Still the thought crossed her mind from time to time.

Alexander knew she turned the heads of just about every man in the Zartonian Galaxy but she was looking for something extra special; a man of Christian integrity and strength. Someone that can be a leader for the kingdom as well as the family. Separating suitor from pretender was a true full time job for Alexandria. She had to be careful not to let just anyone into her inner circle.

After the handmaidens finished attending to her needs, Alexandria prayed then went to bed. Completely exhausted from the week's activities, she quickly drifted off to sleep.

For the first time in many years there was calm and quiet around the palace and throughout Kadesh. No fighting, gunfire, or deaths but finally peace in Alexandria's kingdom.

5

The shuttle bay in Quetal was full of spectators and dignitaries as the warriors prepared to leave for their trip to Neptonia. It was a very beautiful and joyous day in which pictures were taken and well wishes were given.

The High Council along with Governor Lenny were all dressed in their best and waved at on lookers as they prepared to enter their shuttle. Privately, even the Generals were glad they relented. To see the thousands of on lookers, banners and cheers were all worth giving in to the military regulations. People were having fun again and the warriors were achieving legendary status. No one could ever have imagined this day.

The crowds were anxiously awaiting the entrance of the Galactic Warriors. The shuttle for the future newlyweds was off in the corner of the bay and heavily guarded. Not so much guarded for danger but for crowd control. There were so many spectators inside and outside of the launching bay, that even the short so yard walk from the elevator to the shuttle would be hectic.

Now the warriors were exiting the elevator and the crowd erupted in cheers. Security personnel cleared a path to the shuttles. Along the way there were many handshakes and pats on the back.

There seemed to be more people for this send off then the arrival from Kech. It was exciting yet exhausting as they fought back the crowds.

Once everyone made it to the shuttle, everyone collapsed into their seats from fatigue. They felt as though they just went through another war. One could only imagine what would be awaiting them on Neptonia.

"This is shuttle Galactic awaiting clearance for takeoff" said "Buck"

After a few moments, a voice responded.

"Shuttle Galactic you're cleared for takeoff." "Ok everyone strap in" said "Buck"

As the shuttle pulled out of Nebulan's atmosphere and into outer space, everyone began to move around and conversed.

"Well guys this is it! Last day of freedom for 4 warriors" said Wally

Everyone chuckled at the remark because they knew Wally wanted to use this as a reason to throw a bachelor party.

"Yes it seems like a dream. I still can't believe how we were blessed to get the council to sign off on it" Said Reginald. "Yea we really need to show our appreciation to Queen Alexandria for sticking her neck out for us. She's a very good person" said Mariana.

Everyone nodded in agreement and was thinking of what they could for Alexandria.

"I'm not sure if we could ever do anything to repay her kindness, but I suggest that we all honor her with a gift from the warriors" said Arnold. "That's a great idea Arnold. We've received so much and we owe her our lives" said Regina.

"DD" looked at Regina and nodded with a wide eyed smile on his face. Everyone was pondering what to give Alexandria and how to present it to her. But whatever happened, they knew that she would very much appreciate it.

"So Akasha, what are you going to give the queen?" asked Regina.

Akasha began to rub her forehead and turned away from Regina.

"I don't know man. She might have to wait till payday cus my credits are kinda slim right now" said Akasha.

Regina looked at Akasha sternly and reached over and turned her around. She looked directly into her eyes with harsh anger. Akasha has never seen this look in Regina's eyes. For the first time, Akasha showed fear.

"You better open up your 15 year old heart and show some appreciation! Do you hear me child!" said Regina in an angry motherly tone.

Akasha was very much surprised because Regina normally had a very laid back nature. But becoming a wife was changing her attitude. Regina realized that she not only had to be a wife to "DD" but also a corporal in this unit. In addition, Akasha was going to be living with her and she truly needed a mother figure in her life. Although Akasha was intelligent and talented, she needed a great deal of guidance. Regina figured now would be the perfect time to start setting boundaries.

"Ok. Ok. I promise to find something" said Akasha in a more humble tone.

For the first time sarcasm wasn't in her voice as she recognized Regina was completely serious. The entire unit was caught off guard by Regina's words and attitude. But in everyone's mind, they figured it was about time that someone put Akasha in her place.

Afterward, Regina returned her attention back to "DD' Walking over and sitting in his lap, he snuggled her close in his huge arms and whispered in her ear.

"Hey does anyone know what it's like on Neptonia?" I've heard stories but does anyone know anything about their cities?" asked Wally

Everyone looked at each other in curiosity and blank stares but no one knew anything about the city in which they were going.

"Of course none of us know firsthand, but I remember few years ago a former slave of the empire telling my father that everything on that planet is 4 to 5 times bigger than anything we have on Nebulan. The palaces, the aircraft, even civilian houses are enormous. I also remember him saying the weather was always damp and there was never much sun. A person could sense evil all around them and it was nothing really to write home about" said "Buck"

Everyone became quiet with "Buck's" words. They seemed like words straight from a horror film. Now everyone's perception of Nebulan had been changed. The thoughts of this large, fairytale like world had been shattered.

Mariana and Regina look at each other and shook their heads because this wasn't the backdrop that they envisioned for their wedding.

"That don't seem like a plant but more like a 20th century haunted house" said Akasha. "I agree to the 10th power" said "DD" "How can anyone live on something like that?" "Well guys it makes you appreciate the beauty that we have on Nebulan. Not many planets in the Zartonian Galaxy have the beauty of springtime, the warmth of summer, the brown colors of fall, and the wonderful snows of winter as we do. We're blessed and very fortunate to have every season that God created. Nebulites are a very special race of people that enjoy the fruits of their labors. King Barabas wanted Nebulan more out of jealousy than conquest. With him coming from a planet with that type of description, I guess I can understand why he was always angry" said Reginald

His words brought reflection and understanding to the unit. They truly realized how blessed they were to have the privileges and freedoms that are easily taken for granted.

"That's why I agree with presenting Alexandria with a gift because she has all of the great things. It's the little things that will make the most difference in her life. As a matter of fact, let's do this right. Sergeant Harris make a landing on Kech. I want all of us to to buy one small item for this presentation. Agreed?" said Reginald. "Agreed" everyone responded.

Kech was the final planet before reaching Neptonia. King Barabas had argued that Kech was an escaped moon of Neptonia and wanted to reclaim it in the name of the empire. It was never known if this was true or if Barabas just wanted to use it for a reason of conquest. But what is known is that the orbit of Kech affects the weather conditions on Neptonia. Astronomers on Kech have been studying that for years but have no concrete conclusion because until now no one has been able to perform tests on Neptonia. But scientists on Kech are excited because the treaty opens the possibilities to perform new tests and receive data from Neptonia.

After completing their shopping on Kech, the warriors began the final miles to Kech. Everyone was excited and curious as to what they would see on Neptonia. This would be their first time on Neptonia and everyone was anxious to see if "Buck's" information was accurate. They were young and had teenage like curiosity. As they approached Neptonia, a voice cam over their intercom system;

"Shuttle Galactic. This is Sergeant Troy of Neptonia ground control. We have you on radar. Continue on your present course and speed to the Royal Palace landing Bay. Welcome to Neptonia and enjoy your stay." " Roger that Sergeant. We appreciate that warm welcome. Galactic out" responded "Buck" "Ok guys strap yourselves in. We're making our approach and this could get bumpy. Radar is picking up some severe storms ahead"

As the shuttle made its way into the fierce Neptonian atmosphere, it was met with severe lightning and wind which caused great turbulence to their shuttle. "Buck", who is always cool under pressure, guided the ship with expert and steady hands. He maneuvered the ship through the storm to the landing area. As he approached, the roof on a large dome building opened to receive them.

After landing, everyone looked at their surroundings from the shuttle windows. Everyone's eyes expanded as they gazed upon the largest star fighters that they had ever seen. As they continued to look in amazement, they almost didn't notice a welcoming committee approaching the shuttle.

The Committee was led by Prince Darnell, who was anxious to once again see his father. As the warriors exited the shuttle, Reginald greeted his son with a hug.

"Son it's so good to see you again" said Reginald. "And I you father "responded Darnell. "Of course son you remember my fiancé Mariana?" asked Reginald "But of course" responded Darnell as he kissed the back of her hand. "Ms. Woods it's always a pleasure to make your acquaintance."

"Oh no Prince please call me Mariana." "Only if you promise to call me Darnell." "Agreed" said Mariana as she hugged her future step son.

"Please everyone follow me and I'll show you to your chambers. I know that you must be tired" said Darnell.

Darnell led each person to their own room and assigned them a personal servant that attended to their every need. All of the warriors marveled at how large and beautiful the palace was. They had never seen so many different types of rubies and gems in their life. The hallway and corridors were spacious enough for all to walk through side by side.

Their rooms contained king sized canopy beds, lined with satin sheets and pillow cases. All had their own bathrooms, dens, and flatscreens monitors. Also their windows overlooked the whole city of Kadesh. Out of the windows they could see the tall skyscraping buildings, busy shuttle traffic, and the bright lights that lit up the night sky.

The warriors were star struck with everything that they saw. Everything that they had been told about Neptonia was true but to see it with their own eyes gave them a deeper respect for the Neptonian Empire.

"Well everyone make yourselves at home. Mother will meet you in one hour at the royal chapel. I shall return for you then" said Darnell "Father. A word please."

With that everyone settled into their rooms while still marveling at the size and high ceilings. Never in their wildest dreams did they ever think that they would be staying at the Neptonian palace.

"Father I would be honored if you would join me for refreshment in the dining chamber." "Of course son. It would be my pleasure" said Reginald

As they made their way to the dining hall, Darnell showed Reginald his many scholastic achievements and military metal that were encased in glass on the highway walls. It seemed at each turn there were more metals and honors. Reginald looked at each achievement with pride, remembering the many metals that his father has lining the halls of the capital building in Quetal. He remembers walking the halls with his father and also thinking of how brave he was.

The stroll had so many memories and he quickly realized that Darnell had greatness in his blood.

"Father are you ok?" Darnell asked with concern.

Reginald, who had drifted into a trance, came to himself.

"Sorry son. I was thinking of how much you remind me of your grandfather. He was the greatest fighter pilot that Nebulan ever knew. You would have loved him" said Reginald.

As they took their seats at the table, servants came and served them tea and placed a tray of fruit in the center. It was an elegant table with unusual china, gold centerpieces and silverware that shined like diamonds; a perfect place for a relaxing conversation.

"So father, tell me more about my future stepmother. You two are getting married tomorrow and I feel that I hardly know her" said Darnell. "Well son aside from being tall and beautiful, Mariana is very intelligent and hard working. She knows how to be a soldier and a lady at the same time. But the most attractive thing about her is that she's God fearing. Mariana truly loves the Lord and has stuck by me through thick and thin. A man can't ask for much more than that" said Reginald. "You know father, Mariana truly handled the situation with the three of us with class and maturity.. Most women her age would have thrown in the towel and walked away but she listened, learned, and trusted your love for her. For me father, that was impressive" said Darnell. "Thank you son, I have to say it's not going to be easy juggling career and marriage; but I've made a vow that I will never put my career ahead of family. That always spells disaster in the end when a man does that. Remember it always God, family, then career. No exceptions" said Reginald. "You're my son and anytime you want to come visit then come. I will never be too busy for you." " Thanks father. It's very much appreciated and knows that you and Mariana are welcomed here anytime.

As they sat at the table and continued to enjoy each other's company, they really that they had so much in common.

Prince Darnell completely lost track of time and remembered he needed to get the warriors and the dignitaries to the chapel for a dress rehearsal.

After getting all of the parties together, he led them to the church where Alexandria was waiting for them.

On first glance, everyone noticed the beauty and majesty of the room. It was decorated with grace and elegance. The floor was covered with red carpet and roses lined the ends of the pews. Gold statues of Alexandria were on each corner of the room; each statue contained a different verse of the bible. At the center of the room where the bride and groom meet, was podium with a gold bible placed on it.

No expense was spared. All of the guests were simple amazed by what they saw.

Regina and Mariana were brought to tears with the beauty of the chapel. This is what they envisioned on their wedding day, hugging each other with happiness and joy.

Alexandra and her hand maidens were at the center of the room and Slaughter was speaking to members of the High Council. The allied governors were being entertained by Prince Darnell, whose social skills had grown quickly since receiving his father.

"Alexandria this chapel is so beautiful. We just can't thank you enough for making this day so special" said Mariana. "Yes you have really made this a time that we'll never forget" said Regina.

Both had tear-filled eyes as they continued to look around the chapel.

"Ladies it's my honor and my gift to you and your gentleman. I want you to know that our friendship will last long after your wedding day had come and gone" You are more than friends; you're my family. Anytime, anywhere you need me. I'm always just a transmission away. Understand?" " Yes we understand and that works both ways your highness" said Mariana.

Alexandria motioned for two of her hand maidens to join her.

"These are my handmaidens. From this point forward, anything you need they will provide for you" said Alexandria. "Thanks a million" said Regina.

This was all uncharted territory for the warriors. They had never been exposed to royal treatment or a wedding.

Alexandria had put everyone in their places and was about to perform a wedding rehearsal with the pastor and the wedding court.

"Reginald who's going to be your best man?" asked Alexandria." I would be honored if my son would stand up for me. If it's ok with him of course?" said Reginald.

An immediate smile went across Darnell's face.

"It would be my honor to stand with you father."

"Darrell who will stand with you?" asked Alexandria. "Well if it's all the same with you your highness, I have three men that I would like to stand with me. Arnold, Wally, and " Buck" would you stand with me on the greatest day of my life? "said "DD

All three stood up and joined him at the altar.

"Of course we will" said Wally.

All three shook hands with "DD" and assumed their positions.

"Finally, Regina and Mariana. Who's to be your matron of honor?"

They both looked at Akasha and smiled.

"We'll have Akasha stand for both of us you highness" said Regina.

This brought a big smile to Akasha's face because for once she felt useful and not a liability. Regina reached down and hugged her shoulders which really built up Akasha's self confidence.

Meanwhile, Alexandria continued to rehearse and make sure that the flowers, music, etc where all perfect. It was so important to her that everything was perfect.

In the absence of fathers, General Thomas and General Gordon were chosen to give the brides away. This was an extreme honor for both of them and probably the only time anyone had seen them blush.

After two hours of rehearsal, Alexandria felt comfortable that everyone knew their assignments. One would wonder if she was preparing the warriors for marriage or putting out ideas for her future wedding.

After briefing everyone concerning seating and arrival times, she led everyone in a short prayer and dismissed for dinner.

"Grooms bid your brides farewell for they will spend the remainder of the evening with me" announced Alexandria. "You will reunite with them tomorrow at 2p.m."

Everyone was lead to the dining chambers by palace servants.

The tables were extremely long and very well decorated. Each seat contained nameplates, champagne glasses, silverware, and gold plates. The entire room shined from the decorative gems on the walls and high ceiling lights. The look on everyone's faces told how impressed everyone was with Neptonia's hospitality.

Everyone was all laughs and smiles as they strolled around the room looking at paintings of all of the former kings and queens of Neptonia.

Now Alexandria had not yet arrived. Being fashion conscious, she wanted to dress accordingly but yet not take the focus off the guests of honor.

"May I have your attention everyone? It is our honor to present to you Queen Alexandria."

On point, Alexandria entered the room escorted by Prince Darnell. She was decked out in a in a long flowing blue sparkled dress with matching earrings. Her jewelry sparkled as much as her dress. Her presence demanded attention as Darnell seat her at the end of the table.

Servants made sure that all champagne glasses were filled and accommodations taken care of. This was a gala event that no one would ever forget. This night made all of the rigors of war worthwhile.

"I'd like to raise a toast" said Captain Slaughter. "The Neptonians and the

Nebulites have fought many battles and fought well. Even during war we had great respect for the Nebulite bravery and courage. But I thank God that I've lived long enough to raise my glass to peace and love. To Peace and Love!!"

Everyone raised their glasses and repeated those words of peace and love.

"As prince of Neptonia, it's my honor and duty to say a few words towards the happy couples. I have to say that it's amazing what brings people together. Only a God given miracle can turn hatred into unity in such a short amount of time. Through this war, I learned a great deal about Nebulan, but more importantly I learned a great deal about life. Life has brought two couples together and life has brought me a father. So it's with great pleasure that I lift my glass to these happy couples. I wish you continued success and happiness."

As everyone was drinking to Prince Darnell's toast, the servants began bringing in the main course which consisted of ribs, catfish, macaroni cheese, green beans, along with dinner rolls. The feast was elegantly spread on the table and the aroma watered everyone's taste buds.

There was total surprise because everyone expected finger foods but Alexandria had her cooks work for days preparing this meal.

As the tops were taken off and the food displayed, the appetites grew even greater. Everything looked perfect and no one was disappointed.

"Allow me to give a final toast. I want to thank God for the honor of seeing my friends pledge their lives to each other. I want to also thank the Governors and High Council for making this day possible. We are all family so let's raise our glasses to family" Said Alexandria.

As the evening progressed, everyone continued to eat, drink, and conversed. There was joy and sincerity in every word and in every handshake. It seemed that this was a new beginning in every aspect. There was laughter and dancing all around the room.

The happy couples were enjoying their last moments together before separating with Alexandria and Darnell.

Inside the warriors were wishing that their parents could see this day. But they also knew that this was their time because they were the new beginning for Nebulan; as Alexandria and Darnell was the new beginning for Neptonia.

6

The big day had finally arrived and excitement rang out all over Neptonia. On this day, April 29, 5012, all work in the city of Kadesh was halted and a holiday declared. It was Alexandria's wish to have as many citizens as possible witness this historic event.

Accommodations were made for everyone. For example, jumbo monitors were placed outside of the palace walls for those not able to be seated in the chapel. Telecasts were made available for home viewers and shuttle pickups were being arranged for elderly Neptonians.

This was unlike any day in Neptonia's history. Never had the royal palace been made available to ordinary citizens and never had there been such camaraderie. Love could be felt all over the planet. Even the sun was peeking through the normally stormy climate of Neptonia. One could feel the warmth of the rays and see the clouds brighten as the sky brightened. No one could have envisioned a more perfect day for a wedding.

On the inside of the palace, flowers and decorations lined the halls as well as the chapel. Servants, military personnel and handmaidens were all dressed in their best which added to the décor of the palace.

Everyone was mingling throughout the palace. Small talk, handshakes, and joking could be heard at every turn. It seemed that everyone was enjoying the moment and learning more about the Neptonian culture.

Alexandria took peaks from her chamber doors to see how everyone was getting along. She was so pleased and relieved that the Hedera Solar

System was finally united. People who were once enemies were now sharing drinks and food with one another.

Alexandria's eyes began to water as she looked over the crowd. A long motherly smile came across her face as she took everything in. She remembered her mother would always say to her during childhood. "Alexandria, you're going to be the one to bring change the empire."

Of course as a child, she would never believe this. But now Alexandria understood that her mother, Queen Bethesda, saw a better day through her.

"Lord I thank you for this special day. I pray that my parents are resting in peace knowing that Neptonia and Nebulan are happy and free" said Alexandria with tears flowing down her cheeks.

"Are you ok?" asked Regina with a look of concern. She didn't understand the true sentimental value in Alexandria's heart.

"Yes ladies I've never been better. Spending the night with you has allowed me to feel that I know you much better." " We feel the same way. Thank you for your generosity and hospitality. You're more like a big sister to us" said Mariana.

They shared in a group hug in the middle of the queen's chambers. It was no ordinary embrace but one that signified a pact that would never be broken. Alexandria then returned to the table and sipped some orange juice that had been a part of their breakfast.

In the previous night, the three of them stayed up and shared stories of their lives and watched romance movies on the flatscreen. Surprisingly little was said regarding the wedding. It was mostly time spent bonding and learning about one another.

"Mariana and Regina joined her at the table helping themselves to juice and sandwiches. Nerves had started to set in as they looked to the wall and saw that it was noon. Alexandria noticed their change in body posture and the fact that they had grown quiet.

"Ladies allow me to first say that it has been my honor to share in the greatest day of your lives. In exactly two hours, your lives will change forever. All of the dignitaries, Neptonians, Nebulites, and others will watch you not only pledge your lives to the men that you love but also bring two worlds together. Of course never having been married, I can't give you advice in that area. But what I can do is tell you to never stop feeling the way you do right now. Never allow marriage or love for you husbands grow old. Happiness is often searched for but very rarely found. Treat it like a royal jewel.

Per hands on their shoulders, she began to speak as a mother would to a daughter.

"Never forget that you can call me at anytime. At age 31, I can give you advice about experiences that you haven't had yet."

After laughing at her last comment, Mariana looked directly into Alexandria's eyes as if something was on her mind to say. She looked down at her plate then her eyes returned to Alexandria.

"Is there something on your mind Mariana?" asked Alexandria.

Mariana took a deep breath as if to motivate herself to speak.

"Alexandria before I walk down that aisle, there is something that I must ask you" "What is that my dear?" "We discussed this back on Kech, but I need to hear it from you one more time for my own well being" said Mariana.

Alexandria once again looked at her in motherly fashion then grabbed her hand.

"What is it sweetie?" "I need to hear again where your heart is concerning Reginald."

Alexandria smiled as she looked at both Mariana and Regina. She knew they were young and never before been in love. It almost escaped Alexandria that Mariana was about to be a stepmother to her son and needed reassurances that no interference would come to her marriage.

"Mariana remember this; My feelings for Reginald are only as a man that is a father to her son. Yes I loved him once but that was many moons ago. His heart is focused on you and mine on my kingdom. You have my word as a Neptonian that no interference will come to you or your marriage. Sleep soundly and know that you'll never have to look over your shoulders."

Alexandria came around the table and gave her a hug. "Feel better" asked Alexandria. "Yes it's forever settled in my mind and heart" said Mariana. "Great! Now it' time to prepare you ladies for the greatest day of your lives"

Alexandria called in her hand maidens and had them escort the ladies to separate bathrooms. There they received scrub downs, massages, new hairstyles, gold earrings and two of the most beautiful wedding dresses that they had ever seen. The dresses sparkled from the diamond clusters that lined the front of the dresses.

As they sat, handmaidens put just the right touches of makeup on their faces and brushed their hair until it was just right. Regina's hazel eyes were brightened as she looked at her shoulder length hair being styled. Neither had worn makeup nor been made over before. As they looked at themselves in the mirror, they began to feel more like royalty than soldiers. They could barely recognize themselves as they looked starry eyed at themselves.

Much to the frustration of her handmaiden, Mariana would continuously run her fingers through her hair and she would constantly have to rebrush it.

"You have such beautiful long hair my lady; but you must leave it in place and allow your husband the opportunity to run his hands through it" said the handmaiden with a smile. "Oh I'm sorry. I just never knew that my blond hair could look so perfect" said Mariana. "Remember that 20th century movie called Cinderella?" asked Regina. "Yes" "That's what we look like at this moment in time. Honestly I'd like to look and feel like this every day. For the first time in my life, I actually feel like a lady" said Regina as she continued to look starry eyed into the mirror." "I agree" said Mariana.

A few minutes later a knock came to the door. Alexandria peeped in.

"Ladies it's time"

As she looked in, Alexandria saw two completely different looking women. They no longer looked like soldiers, but young ladies about to become wives.

"Wow! You ladies are so beautiful. I know two guys that are going to be very impressed. Are you ready?" "Yes" They answered nervously. Their military training taught them not to give into fear but they never experienced the type of emotions that they feel now.

All of the guests had arrived and been seated. The pastor, the grooms, and the entire wedding party were in place. All that was missing was the arrival of Alexandria.

Everyone stood as she entered through a side door escorted by Captain Slaughter and followed closely by handmaidens. Her throne was in the center of the room directly behind the alter.

As she sat and her hand maidens stood behind her throne, everyone else returned to their seats. Captain Slaughter stood at her side and gave a nod to the priest for him to begin the ceremony. At that moment soft music began to play and through the doors came flower girls who were pitching red roses onto the carpet. They beautifully blended in with the red carpet and the flowers that were lining the pews.

As the flower girl took her place across from the grooms, Akasha entered through the door wearing a light blue silk dress and carrying a bouquet of red roses in her hands. With her dress and French rolled hairstyle, Akasha looked more of a woman in her mid 20's than 15. She smiled nervously as she made her slow march down the aisle.

"Shall we all stand for the entrance of the brides?" said the priest.

At once everyone stood as the musicians played the wedding march. Smiles instantly came on to the faces of Reginald and "DD" as they prepared to receive the loves of their lives.

First was General Thomas escorting Mariana who had her eyes completely fixed on Reginald. Her walk was slow and elegant. She took a brief moment to look up at Alexandria who was all smiles. Thomas placed Mariana's hand in Reginald's and gave him a pat on the back.

Regina made her entrance escorted by General Gordon. Already 5'8, she really towered over the general in her high heels. " DD" gave her a big grin as she made her way down the aisle. She remembered how they would resort to name calling rather than say how much they liked each other. As they held each other's hands before God and witnesses, both were looking deep into each other's eyes and reminiscing.

As the vows were being given and exchanged, people could be seen taking pictures and making videos of this historic moment. Everyone wanted to make sure to soak in as much as this historic moment as possible.

"The rings please" said the priests.

The grooms place the rings on the bride's fingers and repeated their vows as did the ladies. Both were nervous as they repeated the priest's words.

"Having exchanged your vows before God and witnesses, understanding that these rings are a symbol of faithful and unending love, I now by the power invested in me by the Neptonian Empire, pronounce you husbands and wives. Gentleman, you may kiss your brides."

While they were kissing, everyone stood and applauded.

"I now present to you Mr. and Mrs. Terry and Mr. and Mrs. Dawson" the priest announced.

The musicians once again played as the guests of honor made their way through a cloud of rice and into the reception chambers. There was a mountain of food and drinks awaiting everyone. Beautiful tables were set for the guests and a special area was set apart for Alexander and the wedding party.

It was a grand evening as toasts were made, people danced, and everyone just had a great time. The room was dimly lit with a romantic atmosphere that made romance very easy to put on display.

"Well Mariana we did it" said Reginald as he fed her a piece of shrimp.

"Yes we did and I truly thank God for allowing this to happen. I know that I'm young but I promise to do my best to make you happy each and every day" said Mariana. "Mrs. Terry you really looked beautiful out there today. Not that you're not a beautiful woman, but today you truly looked special." " Thank you my love" said Mariana.

Mariana reach over and gave Reginald a passionate kiss. They felt relieved that after all these years, it was time to finally exhale and enjoy each other without hiding.

"Well "DD" you're stuck with me now my brotha" said Regina with a big grin. "Well Gina I wouldn't have it any other way. I just pray that you don't snore at night" said "DD" " Well my big strong handsome man you have about 200 years to get used to it" said Regina.

"DD" laughed and put his arm around his wife and brought her face to his chest. It would seem that the four of them were in their own world and nothing else mattered.

It was truly a beautiful night for the newlyweds. One that they wished would never end. Having their lives begin at a place where it easily could have ended made the night even more special.

The crowd was thinning as the evening grew late. Before leaving Alexandria and Darnell said their good bye's to the newlyweds.

"We understand that you guys want to leave tomorrow for your honeymoon. Well as our last gift to you, we will have a shuttle ready to take you to Argon in the morning" said Alexandria. "Thank you your highness for everything. To be honest we could not thank you enough for what you've done for us" said "DD" "You guys just be happy. That's enough repayment for us" said Darnell. "Well in that case son, Neptonia will be paid in full" said Reginald jokingly. "Well we're going to retire for the evening. Please continue to enjoy yourself. This is your night" said Alexandria.

The warriors continued to dance and chat well into the early morning hours after everyone had long left. They were just too excited to sleep and no one wanted the night to end.

"Akasha baby its 2a.m. Time for you to hit the clouds" said Regina.

Normally Akasha would rant and rave but after today she found a new respect for Regina who was now assuming the role of wife and big sister.

" Ok. If I miss ya'll in the morning , have a safe flight" said Akasha as she hugged the newlyweds.

"Arnold, Wally, "Buck", we want to thank you guys for standing up for us. You're the greatest men that we know" said Reginald. "No problem. Maybe one day some girls will feel sorry for us and you guys can return the favor" said Arnold, which brought laughter to the group. "Anytime. Anywhere." added "Buck" "You guys just enjoy yourselves and don't worry about a thing while you're gone. Just take a few dives in the ocean for ol Wally." "Sure thing my brotha" responded "DD"

About 30 minutes later, fatigue hit everyone and they decided to call it a night. It was an evening that they would never forget.

This was truly a new beginning for them; the ending of the legacy left by their parents and the beginning of their own. Finally there was unity. No more Neptonia vs. Nebulan but now they will be one galaxy under one treaty.

A new beginning, a new life, and a new legacy.